WIN A BAGFUL O' CASH
WITH YOUR BAGFUL O' CHICKEN
in our
$99,999.99 BAGFUL O' CASH
CHICKEN CHALLENGE

It's the chance of a lifetime! Eat Chicken in the Bag at every one of our fine franchises in a period of sixty days. If you're the first to do it, you'll win the $99,999.99 Bagful o' Cash—and a penny for your thoughts.

Suddenly I understood. "You mean we're going to try to win this contest?"

Dr. Prechtwinkle's teeth flashed like a shark's. "I'll take care of the transportation. You'll take care of the eating."

"But that's crazy! There must be a couple hundred of these places. There's no way I'm going chicken all summer long for breal ner!"

"No? Well, how else do you forty-nine thousand, four hundr and thirty-seven cents you owe camera?" Dr. Prechtwinkle deman

"I'm thinking it over," I said.

Bantam Skylark Books of related interest
Ask your bookseller for the books you have missed

BANANA TWIST by Florence Parry Heide
BE A PERFECT PERSON IN JUST THREE DAYS!
by Stephen Manes
BONES ON BLACK SPRUCE MOUNTAIN
by David Budbill
THE CHOCOLATE TOUCH by Patrick Skene Catling
GEORGE'S MARVELOUS MEDICINE by Roald Dahl
IT'S NEW! IT'S IMPROVED! IT'S TERRIBLE!
by Stephen Manes
JACOB TWO-TWO AND THE DINOSAUR
by Mordecai Richler
LIZARD MUSIC by D. Manus Pinkwater
NUTTY FOR PRESIDENT by Dean Hughes
TOP SECRET by John Reynolds Gardiner

The Third Strange Thing That Happened to Oscar Noodleman

CHICKEN TREK

by Stephen Manes
illustrated by Ron Barrett

A BANTAM SKYLARK BOOK®
NEW YORK · TORONTO · LONDON · SYDNEY · AUCKLAND

RL 3, 007–011

This edition contains the complete text
of the original hardcover edition.
NOT ONE WORD HAS BEEN OMITTED.

CHICKEN TREK
A Bantam Skylark Book/published by arrangement with E.P. Dutton

PRINTING HISTORY
E.P. Dutton edition published August 1987
Skylark Books is a registered trademark of Bantam Books, a division of Bantam
Doubleday Dell Publishing Group, Inc. Registered in U.S. Patent and Trademark
Office and elsewhere.

Bantam edition/August 1989

ISBN 0-553-15716-7

Published simultaneously in the United States and Canada

Bantam Books are published by Bantam Books, a division of Bantam
Doubleday Dell Publishing Group, Inc. Its trademark, consisting of the
words ''Bantam Books'' and the portrayal of a rooster, is Registered in U.S.
Patent and Trademark Office and in other countries. Marca Registrada.
Bantam Books, 1540 Broadway, New York, New York 10036.

PRINTED IN THE UNITED STATES OF AMERICA

0 9 8 7 6 5 4 3

for Susan,
with gravy

1

"No more pencils! No more books!" shouted my friend Donald McDonald.

"Yeah, yeah. No more teachers' dirty looks, either. Big deal," was all I could say. Vacation time was no thrill for me. I, Oscar Noodleman, was going to have a terrible summer. A rotten summer. The rottenest summer of all time. There was absolutely no doubt about it.

What made it worse was that Donald was going to have the best summer ever. His rich parents were sending him on the International Junior Monster Tour. He waved the brochure around every time I went to his place.

"Scotland first!" he shouted. "The Loch Ness Monster! Then on to Transylvania for Count Dracula's Castle. Next, the Himalaya Mountains of Tibet. We'll hunt for the Abominable Snowman!"

I looked at the horrible full-color photos. "Sounds great," I admitted.

"There's more! We visit a bunch of famous places where ghosts and werewolves hang out! We end up on the West Coast of the United States. We'll track down Bigfoot, the Sasquatch. What a great summer!"

"I'm glad somebody's going to have one," I said.

"Oh, come on. Maybe your vacation won't be so bad."

"And maybe it'll snow on the Fourth of July."

Donald looked thoughtful. "Hey, I'll be in the Himalayas on the Fourth of July. I bet it *will* snow. Neat!"

"Will you quit rubbing it in?" I said.

"I still say your summer could turn out okay."

"Okay? Spending my entire vacation in Secaucus, New Jersey, working for my second cousin, Dr. Peter Prechtwinkle? What could possibly be okay about it?"

"He's an inventor, right? Maybe you'll get to help him out with some neat invention."

"You've got to be kidding. You know why I have to spend the summer working for him. I dropped his camera out my bedroom window, and it smashed to bits. It was the only one in the whole world, and it was worth forty-nine thousand, four hundred sixty-two dollars and thirty-seven cents. Plus tax."

"Sure, I know. I was there."

"Well, there's no way he's going to let me work on some other neat new invention. What if I dropped it or something?"

"Yeah. I see what you mean. So what kind of work do you think you'll really end up doing?"

"Who knows? Mowing lawns. Making beds. Washing dishes. Cleaning toilets. All I know is it's going to be awful."

3

"Look on the bright side," Donald said.

"What bright side?"

"At least you'll get a lot of neat postcards from my vacation."

I threw one of Donald's three-dollar chocolate chip cookies at him.

2

One week later I climbed aboard a crowded bus
for Secaucus, New Jersey. My mom and dad waved
good-bye through the window. They didn't look too
unhappy to see me go. They were flying to Switzer-
land, so they were going to have a great vacation.
Everybody was going to have a great vacation. Everybody but me. My seat on the bus didn't even tilt
back like everybody else's.

"Phooey!" I muttered.

"And just why is a handsome healthy fellow like
yourself in such terrible rotten shape, sonny boy?"
asked a voice at my ear.

I didn't answer. All I could do was turn and stare.

The woman who plopped down beside me was almost as wide as two seats put together. Her hair was carrot-orange with a blue streak down the middle. Her dress had purple cows all over it. And her breath smelled like she'd just eaten a salami, onion, and garlic sandwich with half a jar of pickle juice for dessert.

"Pleased to meet you, sonny, old friend," she said in a strange accent. "Where you going that you feel so unhappy?"

"Secaucus, New Jersey," I mumbled, trying to move my nose in some other direction.

"Secaucus, New Jersey! Beautifullest place in the U.S. of A.! Where I live, you bet!"

The woman reached under her hat and handed me a little sky-blue card with tiny white stars all over it. The card said:

IS GOLD, YOU BET! TICK AND FLEA COLLAR

SEES ALL— KNOWS ALL
Madame Gulbenkian
FORTUNES AND HOROSCOPES TOLD.
PALMS, TEA LEAVES, FOREHEADS READ.
CRYSTAL BALLS AND CURSES A SPECIALTY!
★ ESTABLISHED FOR OVER 25 YEARS.
(DON'T MISS OTHER SIDE)

I flipped the card over. The other side was white with tiny sky-blue stars. It said:

★ ★ Madame Gulbenkian ★ ★

WISHES, HOPES, AND PROMISES YOU A SPLENDID DAY! IT'S IN THE STARS! 1775 BOULEVARD OF THE PATRIOTS SECAUCUS, NEW JERSEY

Madame Gulbenkian had a very smug look on her face. "Now I know what you going to say next, you bet."

Oh, yeah. Sure she did. I decided to challenge her. "What?" I said.

She handed me a folded piece of notebook paper. Scribbled on it was one word: "What?"

"Did I know, or did I know?" she demanded.

I just nodded. Why do weird things like this always happen to me?

"Now, why you go to beautiful Secaucus?" asked Madame Gulbenkian.

"If you see all and know all, how come you don't know that already?" I asked.

"Don't get snippy with me, sonny person," she huffed. "Maybe I left my crystal ball at home. Maybe you've got sweaty palms. Maybe your forehead is too oily for my sensitive fingertips. Maybe I don't say everything I know. So I would appreciate very much if you would answer my question, please."

I sighed. "I'm going to visit my cousin, Dr. Peter Prechtwinkle."

Madame Gulbenkian gave out a horrible smelly shriek. She snatched up her giant shopping bag and leaped out of her seat. She waddled toward the back of the bus as fast as her legs could carry her. She sat down and glared at me as if I were one of Donald's horrible monsters.

I couldn't figure it out. I didn't think I'd said anything so terrible. I took a look behind me.

Madame Gulbenkian stared back. She mumbled something to herself. Then she pointed her stubby fingers at me as if she were casting an evil spell.

I suddenly felt a throbbing pain in the big toe of my left foot.

3

By the time we got to Secaucus, my toe stopped hurting. But Madame Gulbenkian was still glaring at me and muttering to herself. You can bet I got off that bus in one big hurry.

A tiny helicopter was parked behind the bus. A man with a bushy moustache, a bushy head of hair, and a New York Mets cap stuck his head out the door. "Any Oscar Noodlemans around here?" he whispered in a loud voice.

If my summer was going to start out with a ride in that neat little helicopter, maybe it wouldn't turn out so bad after all. "Me!" I hollered back.

"Not so loud!" whispered the man in the helicopter. Then he shuddered in horror.

9

"I know that's you, Prechtwinkle!" shrieked a smelly voice behind me. "I see all, know all. My eyes see right through disguise, you bet!"

"Come on!" the man whispered louder. "Hurry! Quick!" I grabbed my suitcase and dragged it toward the copter.

Madame Gulbenkian shook her fist at us. "Don't drag that boy into your evil schemes, you nasty Prechtwinkle!" she hollered.

"Toss your suitcase into the WhirlyWhiz and get in!" the man in the helicopter told me.

I did. Then I looked back. Madame Gulbenkian was waddling toward the helicopter in a big hurry. "With this you will never get away!" she shouted.

Dr. Prechtwinkle didn't even glance at her. He handed me a card that said:

DR. PETER P. PRECHTWINKLE

Inventor—Genius—Brain

Blinking lights on the bottom flashed the words:

PLEASED TO MEET YOU

"Fasten your seat belt!" he cried. "We're off!" He adjusted a bunch of knobs, turned a key, and yanked on a big joystick. The WhirlyWhiz chugged, rumbled, and whirred. It belched a cloud of dense black smoke. But it didn't move.

10

"You will never succeed, you bet!" shrieked Madame Gulbenkian. She was so close I could almost smell the pickle juice. But before she could say another word, the WhirlyWhiz took off.

Well, sort of. I mean, it looked like a helicopter, and it sounded like a helicopter. But the Whirly-Whiz kept moving along the ground. It was so slow that Madame Gulbenkian nearly caught up with us! But finally Dr. Prechtwinkle got the copter moving about as fast as a golf cart. And Madame Gulbenkian ran out of breath.

"We've lost her!" Dr. Prechtwinkle cried.

I looked back. Madame Gulbenkian was still shaking her fist at us. But we were pulling away.

We drove awhile. Finally Dr. Prechtwinkle stopped the WhirlyWhiz. He peeled off his bushy moustache. Underneath it was a shiny pencil-thin moustache. He took off his Mets cap and his bushy wig. There wasn't a single hair on his bumpy head.

He stared at me. "I hope you like chicken," he said.

That was not exactly the greeting I was expecting. Most people say "Hello," or "Good to see you," or "Howdy, pardner," or "What's shakin'?" or something like that the first time they meet you. Not Dr. Peter Prechtwinkle.

"Well?" he repeated. "Do you or don't you?"

I shrugged. "Sure. I guess. Chicken's okay."

"Cousin," said Dr. Prechtwinkle, "it is a pleasure to meet you. I am sure we will get along just fine."

I wanted to ask him about his disguise. I wanted to ask him why the WhirlyWhiz wouldn't fly. I wanted to ask him why he was so happy I liked chicken. I especially wanted to ask him about Madame Gulbenkian.

But before I could say another word, my cousin adjusted a knob on the instrument panel. He pushed on the joystick and stomped on one of the pedals. With a puff of white smoke and a horrible roar, the WhirlyWhiz lurched forward again. Still on the ground, though.

4

The WhirlyWhiz made such a racket we couldn't talk. But suddenly Dr. Prechtwinkle shouted "Look!" at the top of his lungs and pointed through the windshield.

We were driving over back roads through a huge swamp. All I could see was brown mud with tall grass sticking up. But then I spotted something huge rising up in the distance.

At first I thought it was the World Trade Center. Then I figured it must be the Empire State Building. Then I was positive it had to be the Statue of Liberty.

But finally I could see what it really was. It was a giant chicken wearing a tuxedo.

Half a minute later Dr. Prechtwinkle grabbed my arm, shouted "Come on!" and dragged me through a door in the giant chicken's belly. Inside was a restaurant, and we found a table all the way at the back. My cousin stuck his finger down on the paper place mat. "Read," he ordered.

I read:

This fine establishment

SPEEDY'S LUNCH

serves

CHICKEN IN THE BAG

The chicken treat that's sweeping the nation!

⅜ CHICKEN (NO GIBLETS)
THAT YOU EAT
WITH YOUR FINGERS

Below that was a chicken wearing a tuxedo with the name "Bagthorpe" on the front. A little balloon over the chicken's head read, "Bagthorpe sez: *It's in the bag!*" The rest of the place mat was a map of the United States. Bagthorpe was pushing a broom across it—"sweeping the nation," I guessed.

The map didn't show any of the places I expected. New York City and Washington, D.C. and Pierre, South Dakota were all missing. But towns like Secaucus, New Jersey and Chillicothe, Ohio and Wahoo, Nebraska were all over the place. Instead of a dot or star, each one was marked by a tiny Bagthorpe.

"Menus?" asked the waitress. She was wearing a cap with a chicken feather sticking out of it.

"No, thank you," said Dr. Prechtwinkle. "One Chicken in the Bag for my cousin here. Nothing for me."

The waitress made a face. "Nothing?"

Dr. Prechtwinkle shook his head. "I do not eat the flesh of dead animals."

"Well, I sure hope you don't eat the flesh of live ones," the waitress replied.

Dr. Prechtwinkle ignored her. He put his index finger on the place mat right below Arizona. "Here. Right here. This is the important part."

WIN A BAGFUL O' CASH
WITH YOUR BAGFUL O' CHICKEN!
in our
$99,999.99 BAGFUL O' CASH
CHICKEN CHALLENGE

It's the chance of a lifetime! Eat Chicken in the Bag at every one of our fine franchises in a period of sixty days. If you're the first to do it, you'll win the $99,999.99 Bagful o' Cash—and a penny for your thoughts!

"So?" I said.

Dr. Prechtwinkle smiled and flipped the place mat over. "Read the rules."

I looked down at the back of the placemat:

OFFICIAL RULES

1. Chicken must be eaten at restaurant. Take-out orders not eligible. Contestants must "clean the bag," leaving nothing but bones. Decision of waiter or waitress is final.

2. Chicken-eating must be certified by restaurant manager on one official contest place mat. Proof must include official Bagthorpe stamp and date.

3. First prize is $99,999.99 plus penny for thoughts and giant Bagthorpe paper sack. Second prize is one-year supply of Chicken in the Bag. Third through one-billionth prizes: the joy of eating America's Favorite Fried Fowl.

4. Prizes not claimed by December 19, 1999 will be donated to chicken research.

5. Winning place mat with all necessary certifications must be delivered in person to International Chicken in the Bag World Headquarters, 12 Pinfeather Lane, Henrietta, TX.

6. Chicken must be eaten by one contestant only. Team entries will be disqualified.

7. Contest not open to employees of International Chicken in the Bag, Inc.; its franchisees; their employees; or chickens. Void where prohibited.

Dr. Prechtwinkle gave me a big grin. "Now, aren't you glad you like chicken?"

Suddenly I understood. "You mean we're going to try to win this contest?"

Dr. Prechtwinkle's teeth flashed like a shark's. "We'll be a team."

"But it says team entries will be disqualified."

"That just means no team eating. I'll take care of the transportation. You'll take care of the eating."

I looked down at the place mat. "There must be a couple hundred of these places. To win, you'd have to eat chicken every day for breakfast, lunch, and dinner."

"No, *you'd* have to. And you forgot snacks."

"You want me to eat chicken three times a day for the entire summer?"

"Sometimes four or five," said Dr. Prechtwinkle.

"But that's crazy! I can't! I won't!"

"Simmer down. You haven't even tasted it yet."

"I don't care if it tastes like my ten most favorite foods all wrapped up in one. There's no way I'm going to eat chicken all summer long for breakfast, lunch, and dinner."

"And snacks," Dr. Prechtwinkle reminded me.

"Right. No way."

"No? Well, how else do you intend to repay the forty-nine thousand, four hundred sixty-two dollars and thirty-seven cents you owe me for breaking my camera?" There was that familiar number again. "Not to mention the tax."

I didn't say a word.

"Well?" Dr. Prechtwinkle demanded.

"I'm thinking it over," I said.

5

What I was thinking was that I never did promise to repay all that money for the camera. The only thing I promised was to work for Dr. Prechtwinkle all summer. And eating chicken three meals every day, plus between-chicken snacks, was not the kind of work I had in mind.

"We'd split the prize fifty-fifty," my cousin said. "Counting the penny, that's fifty thousand dollars for me and fifty thousand for you."

"Hmmmm," I said. That did make it sound a little more interesting.

"And then from your fifty thousand, you can pay me for the camera you broke. I'll forget about the tax."

I did some quick subtracting:

$$\$50,000.00 \text{ (half of prize)}$$
$$-49,462.37 \text{ (for camera)}$$
$$= \text{too hard to do in my head exactly,}$$
$$\text{but not too terrific}$$

"Wait a minute!" I said. "I do all the work, and you end up with all the money?"

"Who do you think is going to pay for all our travel? Not to mention all those chicken dinners at $4.73 each! Et cetera, et cetera. There's more to this than just *eating*, you know."

"I still don't think it's fair."

"You'd end up with $537.63 and the biggest paper sack you've ever seen. Not bad for a summer's work for a kid your age. Remember, you thought you were going to work for me for free."

I thought it over some more. It definitely sounded a lot more interesting than washing floors.

"Is it a deal?" Dr. Prechtwinkle asked.

"Maybe. First I want to see what this stuff tastes like."

"Be my guest."

Just then the waitress arrived. "Cluck, cluck," she mumbled in a kind of bored way. "It's in the bag."

She twirled the feather in her cap. Then she plopped a big brown paper bag right under my nose. A picture of Bagthorpe on it said "Dig in!" A grease stain on it was spreading fast.

I opened the bag and stuck my nose inside. It smelled like plain old chicken, only better.

I reached in and pulled out a leg. It looked like a plain old chicken leg, only prettier.

I bit into the skin. It tasted like—well, it didn't taste a bit like plain old chicken. It tasted absolutely amazing.

"Well?" asked Dr. Prechtwinkle.

The chicken was so wonderful, I couldn't stop eating. "This stuff is great!" I shouted with my mouth full.

"Then you agree to my plan?" my cousin asked.

"I guess," I mumbled through the dark meat. I knew it wasn't polite to talk with my mouth full, but I just couldn't get enough of that chicken.

"Sign here," my cousin said. He handed me a sheet of paper. My fingers turned the page a little greasy as I read:

AGREEMENT

I, Oscar Noodleman, hereby agree, affirm, and swear that if I win the Bagful o' Cash, I will give the following amounts to Dr. Peter P. Prechtwinkle:

$50,000.00 for his assistance in helping me win, and $49,462.37 to reimburse him for the camera I broke.

Dr. Prechtwinkle had already signed. At the very bottom was a blank line with my name printed underneath.

I suddenly thought of a big problem. "Mrrf mf mr mls?" I asked with my mouth full.

"Excuse me?"

I swallowed. "What if we lose?" I repeated.

"Don't say that word!" Dr. Prechtwinkle shouted, turning red in the face. He jumped up from the table. "Don't even think about saying it!"

The waitress hurried over. "What seems to be your problem, mister?"

"I'm quite all right, thank you," he said. He was still shaking a little.

"He doesn't like the word . . ." Dr. Prechtwinkle turned even redder, so I whispered "lose" in the waitress's ear.

She turned to Dr. Prechtwinkle. "Oh, yeah? Why's that, bud?"

"Because if I don't find ninety-seven thousand, three hundred twenty-seven dollars and thirty-six cents in a big hurry, a truly horrible woman is going to do something terrible! Something awful. Something too horrendous to think of!"

"What?" the waitress and I said at the exact same time.

Dr. Prechtwinkle shook his head and sighed. "It's a long story."

"We're listening," said the waitress.

Dr. Prechtwinkle rocked back and forth nervously in his chair. "About a year ago, a woman moved in across the road from my mansion. She dropped in to borrow some bean curd, and we started a conversation. I mentioned that I needed someone to test my Transmogrifier."

"Transmogri-what?" I said.

"The Prechtwinkle Transmogrifier. Model X-17. Highly experimental, you understand."

"What does it do?"

"It turns food into other food. Say your family is having alfalfa sprout casserole for dinner, but you want spaghetti. Put the sprouts in the Transmo (that's what I call it for short). Press a few buttons. In seconds you have a real Italian meal. There's even a microwave oven built in. In fact, it looks just like one."

"Amazing!" said the waitress. "That sounds like something people could really use."

"Did you say that word?" Dr. Prechtwinkle said, breaking into a sweat.

" 'Use!' " I cried. "She said 'use.' "

"Honest," said the waitress.

My cousin sighed and mopped his brow.

"What happened to the Transmo?" I asked.

Dr. Prechtwinkle let out a deep sigh. "Well, it still needed testing. And the woman seemed eager to help. We tried it in my mansion first. We turned my 'Have a Nice Day' mug of herbal tea into a cucumber. We turned the cucumber into potato salad. Then we turned the potato salad back into herbal tea again. The woman said it was the best invention she had ever seen. I took it to her place. I installed it. I went home."

Dr. Prechtwinkle shuddered. "Then I heard the explosion."

"Explosion?" asked the waitress.

Dr. Prechtwinkle nodded sadly. "A loud one."

"Uh-oh," I said.

"I stepped out the front door and looked across the street. There was just a steaming hole where the house used to be."

"Was the woman all right?" asked the waitress.

"She came down a second or two later. Fortunately she landed in a thick part of the swamp. After she got cleaned up, she was just fine."

24

"Was the Transmo all right?" I asked.

Dr. Prechtwinkle shook his head. "Destroyed. To- taled. All gone. My only working model. She had tried to change liver into steak. Apparently the flesh of dead animals was too much for it."

"Then what?" asked the waitress.

"The woman made me sign some papers agreeing to rebuild her place exactly the way it was—except for the Transmo, which she didn't seem to want anymore. It all would have cost precisely ninety- seven thousand, three hundred twenty-seven dol- lars and thirty-six cents. And that would have been no problem, because I was expecting to sell my new video camera, the Prechtwinkle X-1, for plenty of moola. Unfortunately, this second cousin of mine here broke it."

The waitress stared at me and shook her head. "It was an accident," I squeaked.

"If I don't give her the money by Labor Day, this woman will take everything I own. My man- sion, my vehicles, my inventions—everything! I'll be ruined!" He turned toward me. "I might even have to come live with you."

I could just see Dr. Prechtwinkle blowing up *our* house. I tried to hide what I thought of that idea.

"And worse!" my cousin cried. "That woman has threatened to turn *me* into a microwave oven."

"Now, wait a minute," said the waitress.

"It may sound ridiculous to you," said my cousin. "But she's not like other people. This woman has mystical powers. Weird ones."

25

"Oh, come on," said the waitress. "A big fellow like you doesn't believe in such things."

"I didn't used to," said Dr. Prechtwinkle. "But a friend of mine swears this woman turned an uncle of his into an electric blender."

"Come on," I said.

"And I personally know she can cast spells on people. It sounds strange, but every time I see her, my left big toe starts to ache."

A shiver ran down my spine. "Her name wouldn't be"—I pulled the card from my pocket—"Madame Gulbenkian, would it?"

Dr. Prechtwinkle fell backward in his chair. "How did you guess?" he moaned.

I didn't say a word. I borrowed the waitress's pen and signed Dr. Prechtwinkle's agreement. Saving my cousin from Madame Gulbenkian was the very least I could do.

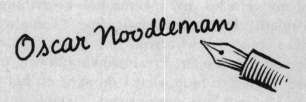

We got the manager to sign my official place mat and stamp it with a little picture of Bagthorpe. Then we took off in the WhirlyWhiz. It didn't make as much noise this time. But it still didn't get off the ground.

"Can this thing fly?" I wondered.

"Of course!" said Dr. Prechtwinkle indignantly. "A few minor adjustments and it'll fly like an ostrich."

"Are we going to use it to try to win the prize?"

"How ridiculous!" said my cousin. "Of course not!"

I looked down at the place mat and tried to count

all the little Bagthorpes on it. I came up with roughly 211.

I did some math in my head and on my fingers. The rules said you had to do the eating in sixty days. That meant I would have to eat Chicken in the Bag three times a day every day, and four times on thirty-one of those days. No matter how you figure it, that's a lot of chicken. But Chicken in the Bag had tasted so great, I figured I could handle the eating part.

But could we really get to all 211 places in just sixty days? A few were in Florida, a couple were in Washington State, and there was even one in Alaska. It seemed like too much traveling for just two months. I asked my cousin about it.

"Remember," he said as we pulled into a drive-way, "you are riding with a genius. And now that we've arrived at my mansion, you'll see exactly what I mean."

I didn't even see what he meant by the word "mansion." The only thing up the drive was a strange boxy building. It looked like two rusty old railroad freight cars set end to end.

Then I happened to look across the road. Off in the distance, I could see an old trailer. Right beside it was a house that looked as though it had been bombed, set on fire, and stomped on by Godzilla. On top was a huge sky-blue sign that was charred around the edges. It had white stars and white lettering that said: **MADAME GULBENKIAN! HERE! STILL OPEN FOR BUSINESS!**

"Hey! You rotten Prechtwinkles over there! I know what you're up to!" screeched Madame Gulbenkian. She slid out all greasy from underneath an old Galaxy convertible. It had sky-blue stars on a white background on the sides, and white stars on a sky-blue background on the hood.

"Ignore that woman!" my cousin cried. "Follow me!"

I grabbed my suitcase, and we walked around the "mansion." Behind it was something like a junkyard. I could see a broken-down donkey cart, an airplane with half a wing, a rusty old steam locomotive, a boat shaped like a car, a car shaped like a boat, and a wrinkly blimp with all the helium let out. There was also a lot of stuff I didn't recognize.

"Would you believe it?" Dr. Prechtwinkle asked. "All these amazing one-of-a-kind vehicles cost me only $128.34."

I could believe it. "Do any of them work?"

"Do they work?" cried Dr. Prechtwinkle. "I will thank you to stop asking such idiotic questions."

I was kind of curious about the locomotive and the blimp. But Dr. Prechtwinkle led the way to what looked like a giant pickle on wheels, complete with warts.

"Get in, get in." He opened the door. "Don't just stand there."

The inside was kind of like a mobile home, with bunk beds, a dinette set, and even a little bathroom. But everything was green. The carpet was green, the ceiling was green, and the walls were green. There were three green paintings labeled **Gherkin**, **Half-sour**, and **Kosher Dill**. A green sign said **EAT MORE PICKLES**.

"What do you think?" Dr. Prechtwinkle asked proudly.

"I've never been in such a pickle," I said.

"Very amusing. This still meets all the standards for an official Picklemobile. It was designed by apes."

"I never knew monkeys liked green so much."

"APES is the American Pickle Education Society," he said with a scowl. Then his eyes began to sparkle. "As you know, regular Picklemobiles are a dime a dozen. But I have personally turned this

Picklemobile into the world's only RemDem^{tm}! In this very vehicle, you and I will be able to dematerialize from this spot and rematerialize anywhere you choose in a matter of seconds. Rome, Moscow, Patagonia, Iceland—you name it."

"You've got to be kidding!" I cried.

"Kidding? I'll show you whether I'm kidding or not! Pick a place!"

I didn't know what to say. This had to be the silliest thing I'd ever heard of.

"Well?" my cousin demanded.

I shrugged. "The moon."

"Has to be on this planet."

I tried to guess where my friend Donald would be right now. I was sure this wouldn't work, but if it did, it would be really fun to surprise him. "Loch Ness, Scotland," I said.

Dr. Prechtwinkle sat behind the wheel and typed on a little keyboard. A panel on the sun visor flashed **LOCH NESS SCOTLAND**. My cousin pulled a big red lever, and loud rumbling noises came from the back. Thick black curtains slid closed around all the windows.

"Never look out while we're in transit," Dr. Prechtwinkle warned. "You could damage your eyes."

The panel flashed **DEMATERIALIZING** . . . Then it read **REMATERIALIZING** . . . Then the rumbling quieted down. The panel flashed **YOU'RE THERE!** The curtains slid open. My cousin pushed the le-

31

ver forward and pointed through the windshield. "Loch Ness, Scotland!" he declared.

All I could see through the windshield was the junk in my cousin's backyard. "How come it looks so much like Secaucus, New Jersey?" I asked.

"It's a well-known fact that Loch Ness and Secaucus look very much alike," he said, fiddling with some knobs on the dashboard. "They're almost sister cities."

I poked my head outside the door and looked around. "*That* much alike?" I asked. I pointed to Madame Gulbenkian's sign across the way.

Dr. Prechtwinkle glanced at the sign and shuddered. Then he shook his head and sighed. "It will just take a minor adjustment," he said, patting me on the shoulder. "You see, in less time than it takes to bake the average potato in a microwave oven"— he shuddered again—"we've actually been to Loch Ness *and back.*"

7

My cousin got under the Picklemobile and banged around. Then he climbed back in and typed **LOCH NESS SCOTLAND** on the keyboard again. He pulled the lever. The rumbling rumbled. The curtains closed. The visor panel flashed.

Then the rumbling stopped and the curtains opened. We were right where we started. We hadn't moved an inch.

Dr. Prechtwinkle did some more banging. We tried again. And again. And again. My cousin claimed we had been to Loch Ness, London, Nepal, Transylvania, and Saskatchewan, and back again so fast we didn't have time to notice. But when we spotted Madame Gulbenkian across the road in Peking, Dr. Prechtwinkle had to admit that the Rem-Dem^{tm} definitely wasn't working right.

"I'm changing our plan," he said. "We'll use the WhirlyWhiz after all."

"But it doesn't even fly!" I reminded him.

"It just needs one or two minor adjustments. The man who sold it to me assured me it can fly like a penguin."

"Penguins can't fly," I said. "And neither can ostriches."

Dr. Prechtwinkle looked as if someone had hit him on the head with a baseball bat. "Really?"

I nodded.

He shook his head sadly. "Never trust a used-invention salesman with a tattoo that says *Born To Deal.*"

"Okay," I said. "But now what?"

Dr. Prechtwinkle scratched his bald dome. "New plan! We will use this vehicle in its Picklemobile mode until I get the RemDem^{tm} working."

He turned the key. The Picklemobile roared into motion. I figured the only reason it worked was that my cousin hadn't invented it.

"Your clever plans will not succeed, you bet!" boomed a voice from a loudspeaker down the road. "You just wait, you betcha!"

"Ow!" Dr. Prechtwinkle and I cried at the very same instant.

He looked at me. "Left big toe?"

34

I nodded.

"Two curses at once, from across the road, yet. She'll probably have to rest up after this," my cousin muttered. "Your toe will recover soon."

35

He reached into his pocket and handed me a picture postcard. "I nearly forgot. This came for you yesterday."

The picture showed a beautiful lake. A monster was drawn in with a marking pen. I flipped the card over. It had come all the way from Scotland. It said:

> Hey, Oscar!
>   Just got here. We're taking the submarine tomorrow. It's going to be great!
>   If I see the Loch Ness Monster, I'll snap a picture for you.
>
> Ferociously yours,
Donald

I was glad to hear from Donald. And I was gladder Dr. Prechtwinkle hadn't invented Donald's submarine. Otherwise, it would probably go straight to the bottom and get swallowed by the monster it was supposed to be chasing.

When you travel in a plain old ordinary car, you watch the scenery. When you travel in a Picklemobile, you're *part* of the scenery.

People point at you. People laugh at you. People pass you just to shout out remarks like "Are you sweet or sour?" and "Wart a dilly!"

Even state troopers want to get into the act. We were driving along, minding our own business. All of a sudden we heard a siren and saw flashing lights behind us.

"We weren't going over the speed limit," my cousin said as we pulled over to the curb. That was certainly true. The Picklemobile couldn't go faster than fifty miles an hour unless you drove it off a cliff.

The trooper came up to the window. "What seems to be the trouble, officer?" Dr. Prechtwinkle asked.

"No trouble," said the policeman. "I just hope I don't have to arrest you for driving a pickle without a license." He laughed as though it was the funniest thing he'd ever heard. Then he tipped his Smokey-the-Bear hat and went away.

"This could really slow us down," I said.

"Don't worry," said my cousin. "By tomorrow the RemDem^{tm} will be running again. Smart alecks won't be able to keep up with us."

I hoped he was right. In one hour, I'd heard enough pickle jokes for a lifetime.

A few jokes later, I spotted a sign that said **EXIT 24, SQUANTZ, 1 MILE**. Then I realized something. "This place mat tells us there's a Chicken in the Bag somewhere in Squantz, Connecticut. But it doesn't say where exactly. We might have to drive all through town to find it."

"Open the glove compartment," said Dr. Prechtwinkle.

I did. A first-baseman's mitt fell out.

"What's this doing here?" I wondered.

"What else would you expect to find in a glove compartment?" Dr. Prechtwinkle asked. "Now look in the very back."

I looked. "All I see is something that looks sort of like a little radio and sort of like a nose."

"Take it out and turn it on."

I did. "What does this radio have to do with finding a Chicken in the Bag restaurant?"

"That is not just a radio. It's the Prechtwinkle ChickenSniffer. Turn it around. There should be one direction where clucking noises come in loud and clear."

I turned it every which way. I turned it upside down and sideways. Nothing.

"I forgot. Pull the antenna all the way out first," said Dr. Prechtwinkle.

I did. The latest hit from my least favorite group, Millard Fillmore and the Dead Presidents, suddenly blared in my ears.

"Give me that!" Dr. Prechtwinkle shouted.

I handed him the ChickenSniffer. He turned down the sound and fiddled with the dial. He pointed the antenna out the window and waved it around. Nothing happened.

"Dead batteries, no doubt," he said. "We'll just have to stop and ask for directions."

We rolled into a neighborhood where a bunch of kids were playing catch in a driveway. Dr. Prechtwinkle stopped the Picklemobile.

"Are you giving away free samples?" one of the kids shouted.

"No!" I shouted back. "Anybody know where we can get Chicken in the Bag around here?"

The kids grabbed their stomachs and stuck out their tongues as if they were going to throw up. "What do you want *that* for?"

"Don't say anything about the Bagful o' Cash," my cousin whispered to me. "They might be spies."

I made up a story. "We heard it was a pretty good place to eat."

"If you like to puke, it is," said one of the kids. "It's called Al's. Up the road about a mile. You can't miss it."

"But you'll wish you had," said one of the other kids.

I thanked them. We hit the road. A minute or two later we found Al's right where it was supposed to be.

But it wasn't shaped like a chicken. The place was just a boxy concrete block building with one sign that said **ALS**.

"They left out the apostrophe," I said.

My cousin didn't notice. He was staring at something else. "Look!"

He pointed to the only other car in the parking lot. It was an old Galaxy convertible. It had sky-blue stars on a white background on the sides, and white stars on a sky-blue background on the hood.

Dr. Prechtwinkle's face suddenly broke out in goose bumps. And I got this tingly feeling that ran from the pit of my stomach all the way down to my left big toe.

We got out of the Picklemobile and walked into Al's. A head of orange hair with a blue streak down the middle was the first thing we noticed.

"Pretend she doesn't exist," my cousin whispered in my ear as we walked past. That wasn't easy.

We sat down. There were no place mats on the table. And when I picked up the greasy plastic menu, I couldn't find the words "Chicken in the Bag" anywhere. I was beginning to think we had come to the wrong place.

The waiter was wearing an apron that said "AL" on it. "What'll it be, folks?" he asked.

Dr. Prechtwinkle lowered his voice so Madame

Gulbenkian couldn't overhear. "One Chicken in the Bag."

"Hey, Al, get this," the waiter shouted to another Al behind the counter. "Another order for Chicken in the Bag!" Dr. Prechtwinkle tried to shush him up.

Too late! "Aha!" cried Madame Gulbenkian. "Just as I suspect, you bet!" Suddenly a piece of paper fell out of her giant shopping bag. She stuffed it back in and tried to hide it, but it was scalloped on the edges, and I knew what it was in a flash. It was an official Chicken in the Bag place mat.

"She's trying for the prize," I whispered to my cousin.

"No!" he shouted with a wild look in his eyes.

I could see why. It would not be easy to beat Madame Gulbenkian. She probably had some powerful tricks up her sleeve. And unless we fixed the RemDem^{tm}, she could get around faster than we could.

And boy, could she eat! Al the Waiter set the bag of chicken in front of her. I timed it on my digital watch: The bag was nothing but bones in exactly one minute and thirty-three seconds.

My bag arrived. "Don't let her show you up," my cousin said in a feeble little voice. But there was no way I could match her if I tried. Besides, it really didn't matter how fast you ate. The important thing was to make sure you ate it all.

But my bag looked kind of funny. The Bagthorpe on it was drawn with crayons. And the chicken in it

43

smelled more like a pigeon that had died three weeks ago.

"This isn't Chicken in the Bag!" I said.

"Of course it is," replied my cousin without even looking. "Dig in."

This chicken was putrid. If I ate it, I was sure I'd get sick. But if I didn't eat it, we couldn't win the prize, and Madame Gulbenkian would turn Dr. Prechtwinkle into a microwave oven.

"Now I know why all those kids made all those faces," I said.

"Wait a second," said Dr. Prechtwinkle. He took out his Swiss army knife and looked at my chicken wing through a little magnifying glass. "Waiter!" he shouted.

Al the Waiter shuffled over to the table. "Can I get you some dessert?"

Dr. Prechtwinkle shook his head. "This is not official Chicken in the Bag. It's greasy, it's smelly, and I'm not sure it's actually chicken at all! In fact, I strongly suspect it's parrot!"

Al started crying. "True, true. Please don't report us."

The Al behind the counter started crying, too. "We fry our best."

"Get it?" Al the First sobbed. "Fry our best? But we're terrible cooks."

Al the Second burst into tears. "Chicken in the Bag International took everything away. The statues of Bagthorpe. The secret recipe. The place mats. The bags."

"Everything!" Al the First agreed. "They took away our franchise! We didn't meet the standards."

"No," said Al the Second. "Not for freshness. Not for juiciness. Not even for unusual atmosphere!"

Suddenly Madame Gulbenkian made a coughing sound. She fell to the floor with an enormous crash. She grabbed her belly and made horrible moans.

"Don't worry about a thing," said Al the First. "We've got a direct line to the local ambulance. They'll take her over to the hospital and pump out her stomach. By morning she'll be good as new. It happens all the time."

My cousin shuddered as he pushed me out the door. "Quick! Now's our chance to lose that crazy woman!"

We jumped into the Picklemobile. Dr. Prechtwinkle kept staring into the rearview mirror as if he expected to see Madame Gulbenkian any second.

I looked back, too, but I was positive we'd shaken her. There was no sign of a Galaxy convertible with stars on it. Our toes felt fine.

"I'm still worried," said Dr. Prechtwinkle. "She'll find us somehow."

"By the time she gets back from the hospital, we'll be hundreds of miles away. How's she ever going to find us?"

"She has ways," said Dr. Prechtwinkle. "How did she find us this time?"

"It's not too hard to follow a Picklemobile," I reminded him.

"Exactly. And until I get the RemDem™ working,

45

we'll still be in this pickle. This is terrible! Awful! If that greedy woman somehow wins the Bagful o' Cash, she'll get all the prize money *and* all my worldly belongings. And then she'll turn me into a microwave oven just for spite!"

It did sound horrible, all right, but I tried to calm my cousin down. "There's no use worrying about it right this minute," I said. "Besides, I'm getting hungry."

"My word, that's right!" cried Dr. Prechtwinkle. "We've got to get you to the nearest Chicken in the Bag before it closes."

The nearest Chicken in the Bag franchise was in a town called Orrington. It was hard to miss. It was on the main road into town, it was shaped like a baseball park, and it was called "Fowl Territory." A big Bagthorpe statue stood guard over the parking lot.

Dr. Prechtwinkle told me to stay in the Picklemobile. He jumped out and began walking around the building. "What are you doing?" I hollered.

He put his fingers to his lips to shut me up, walked all the way around the restaurant, and came back. "Just didn't want any you-know-who's to surprise us," he said. "The coast is clear."

Just as we reached the front door, a hand inside flipped over the little sign that said **OPEN**. What stared us in the face was the back: **CLOSED**.

Dr. Prechtwinkle pounded on the door.

"Come back tomorrow!" shouted a strangely familiar female voice from inside.

Dr. Prechtwinkle pounded on the door some more.

"Don't you understand English? We're closed!" the voice hollered.

Dr. Prechtwinkle kept pounding.

"Stop it!" shouted the voice, but Dr. Prechtwinkle didn't. The hand removed the **CLOSED** sign and peered out at us through the window in the door. Dr. Prechtwinkle started shaking, and I felt pretty creepy myself.

It was Madame Gulbenkian.

10

"Go away!" cried the face in the window.

Dr. Prechtwinkle was speechless. So was I.

"Go!" the woman shouted. "Vamoose! Scram!"

Then I noticed something. The woman didn't have orange and blue hair, she wasn't wearing a dress with purple cows all over it, and she didn't talk with an accent. "That's not Madame Gulbenkian!" I whispered.

"It is, too!" said my cousin. "I'd know her anywhere!"

"Please open the door!" I shouted through the window.

The woman still looked suspicious, but she

opened the door a crack. My cousin was still too stunned to say anything. I had to talk fast.

"Please let us in. We're starving, and I've got to have some Chicken in the Bag. We're contestants in the official Bagful o' Cash Chicken Challenge."

Madame Almost-Gulbenkian threw the door wide open. "Why didn't you say so? I thought you were going to try to sell me some pickles. For my money, there's nothing worse than a salesman. And a pickle salesman is the very sourest kind. As long as you're not pickle salesmen, come on in!"

I followed her through the door. "How did she beat us here?" my cousin whispered.

"I told you. It isn't her," I whispered back.

"It is. She's in disguise," he said.

"I'm telling you, it looks like her, but it's not the same person. She doesn't even talk with an accent."

"She disguised her voice."

"It can't be her," I said. "It just can't be. Quit worrying."

"She'll put poison in your chicken and make your toe fall off," my cousin insisted as we sat down at the table.

The more I looked at Madame Almost-Gulbenkian, the more I began to wonder if my cousin was right. "Two Chickens in the Bag?" she asked, setting place mats down in front of us.

"Just one," I said. "And a Roosta-Cola." Roosta-Cola is a special chickeny-flavored soft drink you can only get at Chicken in the Bag restaurants.

"Anything for him?" she asked, pointing to my cousin.

I shook my head. Dr. Prechtwinkle was shaking all over.

"Is he all right?" asked Madame Almost-Gulbenkian.

"We've had a long drive," I said.

"I know what he needs. A Chicken in the Bag of his very own. On the house."

Dr. Prechtwinkle stood up indignantly. "I do not eat the flesh of dead animals!" he shouted.

"That's no way to talk about my chicken!" cried Madame Almost-Gulbenkian. She marched away in a huff.

I liked the restaurant. It had chickens on the chairs and chickens on the curtains, and it smelled all chickeny. It had official Bagthorpe place mats and the official Bagthorpe statue. Pictures of chickens playing baseball decorated the walls. Everything was fine until Madame Almost came through the swinging door from the kitchen. Then Dr. Prechtwinkle started shaking again.

"Cluck, cluck! It's in the bag!" said Madame Almost with a lot more enthusiasm than the waitress at Speedy's. The paper sack she set in front of me definitely looked official.

"Just one second," said my cousin. He snatched up the bag, stuck his nose in it, and took half a dozen healthy whiffs. Then he reached in for the leg, raised it to his eyes, and squinted at it suspiciously. He did

50

the same thing with the wing, the breast, and the thigh. Then he tossed them back and handed me the bag. "I suppose it's all right."

"All right? I'll say it's all right! I'm the best chicken chef west of Tahiti. Of course it's all right. It's better than all right! Right, kid?"

I nodded. Her Chicken in the Bag was the real thing. I started wolfing it down so fast you might have mistook *me* for Madame Gulbenkian.

Dr. Prechtwinkle was still staring at Madame Almost. "What's eating you, Mister Flesh-of-Dead-Animals?" she demanded.

My cousin didn't answer.

"You remind him of somebody," I said with my mouth full.

"Impossible! The only person in the world who looks anything at all like me is my twin sister Leonora."

Dr. Prechtwinkle coughed, choked, gasped, and sputtered.

"She wouldn't call herself Madame Gulbenkian, would she?" I asked.

"You know her!"

"She is evil itself!" cried Dr. Prechtwinkle.

"Well, I admit her and me don't get along too good, but I wouldn't go that far."

"You're sure you're not in cahoots with her?" said my cousin.

"Cross my heart and hope to be run over by a truck and then have my flesh torn to pieces by rats. We're sworn enemies. She put a spell on me when we were in high school and kept me from getting a date for the prom. I walked around looking like a flounder for a week."

"Then will you help us?" asked my cousin.

We told her the whole story. What Dr. Prechtwinkle wanted her to do was stall her twin if she came in and asked for Chicken in the Bag. Say she was all out. Say she couldn't serve it anymore. Say anything, but refuse to stamp Madame Gulbenkian's place mat. That way, she wouldn't be able to beat us for the Bagful o' Cash and turn Dr. Prechtwinkle into a microwave oven.

"Can't do it," said Madame Almost, whose real name was Juanita Frye.

"Oh, come on," said Dr. Prechtwinkle.

"Nope. For one thing, that would be cheating. For another thing, it might put me in bad with Chicken in the Bag International. And for a third thing, I can't always resist her. When she gets cranky, I can feel it something awful in my left big toe. She learned the trick from one of our uncles when she was a kid."

"Didn't you learn anything from that uncle of yours?" Dr. Prechtwinkle asked.

"One silly little trick. Nothing fancy. I never went in much for that kind of stuff."

Dr. Prechtwinkle looked downhearted. "Come on," said Ms. Frye as she stamped our place mat. "Cheer up. This young fellow here is one fine chicken-eater. And if you lose"—Dr. Prechtwinkle began turning red, but she ignored him—"well, my sister could use a good microwave oven. I know for a fact she's a terrible cook."

11

Some awfully weird things have happened to me. I have helped a bunch of aliens escape from planet Earth. I have been attacked in my very own bedroom by giant squid from the briny deep. But the day that had just passed was as weird as any I had ever lived through.

The night wasn't exactly fun, either. My parents had somehow convinced my cousin that he had to send me to bed by ten o'clock. But there was no chance of falling asleep even if I'd wanted to, because my cousin was up past midnight banging away underneath the Picklemobile. When he sent me to bed, he said he was positive he'd have the RemDem^tm working by morning.

The RemDem™ didn't work the next morning. Or the morning after that. We were stuck with the Picklemobile. And besides eating chicken, there wasn't much to do but look at the scenery. We didn't have a TV set, and the radio didn't work. The only entertainment we had was Dr. Prechtwinkle's one tape cassette: "Pickle Polka Favorites" by Frankie Stankovic and His All-Star Accordion Stinkers. It came with the Picklemobile, and Dr. Prechtwinkle thought it was great.

One day was pretty much like the next. I ate chicken for breakfast. We drove awhile. I ate chicken for lunch. We drove some more. I ate my afternoon chicken snack. We hit the road. I ate my chicken dinner. We rolled down the highway. I ate my chicken bedtime snack. Dr. Prechtwinkle banged around and tried to get the RemDem™ to work. I tried to get some sleep. Then in the morning it started all over again.

Maybe you are wondering how I could keep eating all that chicken. Well, in some places the Chicken in the Bag places were far apart, so some days I only had to eat chicken four times or even only three. Then I could eat anything I wanted for snacks.

But I admit there were times when it started to get to me. I wished I could be eating anything else in the world—18-grain soybean-tofu-bran loaf, carob-covered ants, or even a fast-food hamburger.

Still, eating chicken every meal beat eating what my cousin ate. All his food had to come from health-

food stores. He didn't seem to notice that health-food stores always smell bad—kind of like hospitals or doctors' offices without the alcohol. And his meals smelled even worse. Mostly he lived on a diet of wheat germ, 18-grain cereal, organic carrot tops, unsalted celery seeds, Polish bottled water, and Turkish taffy. He insisted Turkish taffy was nature's most perfect food, if you didn't count what it did to your tooth fillings.

So I got used to chicken. Some people go to jobs where they do the same thing over and over again every day of their lives, and I just figured that was the kind of summer job I had.

What really saved me was dessert. I had dessert at lunch, dinner, between-meal chicken snacks, and sometimes even at breakfast. I had Indian pudding in Maine, peach cobbler in Georgia, milk pie in Wisconsin, and a real feast at a pig-out all-you-can-eat cake bar in Arizona. I had date shakes in California and peanut-butter fudge sundaes in Pennsylvania. Eating chicken five times a day really isn't so terrible if you have the right attitude and dessert.

12

By the time we got to Montana, I had eaten a *lot* of chicken. My place mat was getting so full of Bagthorpe stamps you could hardly see the paper. But Dr. Prechtwinkle was more worried than ever.

"I've got to get that RemDem™ fixed," he grumbled. "Somewhere out there, Madame Gulbenkian is eating her way across the country."

"She can't be ahead of us. I've been eating at least three chicken meals a day. Five most days."

"You don't know her. She's capable of eating eighteen meals a day."

"But she still has to get around to the places. She has to drive just like we do."

"That remains to be seen. That woman will stop at nothing!" said Dr. Prechtwinkle. "She might hire a chauffeur so she can keep going all night long. She might rent a helicopter. With her evil powers, she might ride around on a jet-powered broomstick. For all I know, she might even drive over the speed limit!"

I began to see his point. "Cluck, cluck!" I replied.

"This is serious," he said. "I'm not kidding."

I cackled a little. I didn't want to. I just couldn't help myself.

"No more joking, Oscar, please. I have a lot on my mind today."

I nodded. Then I crowed like a rooster. It was like having laryngitis—only instead of getting hoarse, I got chicken.

Dr. Prechtwinkle glanced at me and slammed on the brakes. He leaned toward me and plucked something from my forehead. "What's this?" he asked, showing me something that looked an awful lot like a chicken feather.

I kind of peeped.

My cousin looked in the rearview mirror. "Uh-oh," he said, and pushed the accelerator to the floor.

I leaned over and looked at myself in the mirror. A couple more featherlike things were sprouting from my forehead. And I couldn't make any human sounds at all. Suddenly I didn't feel so hot. I started squawking like crazy.

"Just hang on. You're going to be all right!" my cousin said. "You'll be all better by lunchtime."

"Lunchtime?" I shouted. "There isn't going to be any lunchtime!" Boy, was I ever glad to have my voice back.

"We have a schedule to keep up!" Dr. Prechtwinkle said.

I looked in the mirror again. The feathers on my forehead seemed to have shaken off. "Don't you understand?" I screamed. "I can't eat more chicken now! I'm turning into a chicken!"

"You were," Dr. Prechtwinkle admitted. "But you're not anymore."

"I'll bet it'll start all over again if I eat one more bagful. This is scary. Just thinking about chicken makes me sick."

"Don't worry," said Dr. Prechtwinkle. "I know exactly what's going on."

"I do, too. I have eaten too much chicken. Way too much. I am not eating another bite. Ever."

Dr. Prechtwinkle looked in the rearview mirror. "Relax. Everything's going to be all right. Don't worry."

Nothing was going to be all right if I had to eat more chicken. I tried to think of an easy way out. But suddenly a starry Galaxy convertible with an orange and blue head sticking up roared past us on the left. It disappeared in a cloud of dust.

"What did I tell you?" demanded Dr. Prechtwinkle. "She *is* driving over the speed limit."

"Maybe she's losing her power," I remarked. "My toe still feels okay."

"Of course your toe feels okay. She put a long-distance chicken curse on you!"

"A what?"

"An evil spell to turn you into a chicken!"

"Come on."

"Lucky for us, a long-distance curse takes a tremendous amount of energy. She can't keep it up very long. That's why she didn't quite turn you into a chicken even though she tried. All that happened was you started clucking a little."

"And grew feathers."

"Don't worry. Now that we know what's going on, we can take precautions."

"What kind of precautions?" I asked.

But before Dr. Prechtwinkle had a chance to an-

61

swer, we spotted Madame Gulbenkian's car pulled over on the shoulder up ahead. A state police car was right behind it. The state trooper at her window jumped in the air and grabbed his left foot.

"Nabbed her!" cried Dr. Prechtwinkle. "Maybe that'll slow her down a little."

"I thought you said she didn't have any energy left for curses," I said.

"That's the last one she'll be giving for a while," my cousin assured me. "Don't you worry."

We probably could have outdistanced her. That would have been fine with me. But Dr. Prechtwinkle had different plans. He parked the Picklemobile just outside Mary's Chickateria. It was a tiny little open-air counter with just three stools and a statue of Bagthorpe.

Madame Gulbenkian drove up, plopped down on the middle stool, and ordered Chicken in the Bag. That's when we made our move. Dr. Prechtwinkle sat down at her left, and I sat down at her right. I ordered a Bag and a Roosta-Cola.

Madame Gulbenkian turned toward me, waggled her fingers, and cackled wildly. I was positive I was going to turn into a chicken again.

But nothing happened. "See?" Dr. Prechtwinkle whispered to me behind Madame Gulbenkian's back. "All out of power. She'll have to recharge herself. There's nothing to be afraid of."

Madame Gulbenkian waggled her stubby fingers at my cousin. "Footsie!" she cried. Dr. Prechtwinkle simply crossed his arms and smirked.

Madame Gulbenkian sulked. "You just wait, you bet," she muttered.

The Bags arrived. Madame Gulbenkian took two whole minutes to turn the chicken to bare bones. Then she wiped her greasy fingers and reached into her shopping bag.

This was the moment we'd been waiting for. Dr. Prechtwinkle got up and stood behind Madame Gulbenkian. I fixed my eyes on her purse. We had her surrounded. We were determined to get a look at her official place mat and find out how well she was doing. There was no way she could hide the mat— or the truth.

"Confidential information," she whispered to the cook, who was also the owner, manager, and waitress. Madame Gulbenkian handed her the place mat facedown.

The second the cook flipped it over, she broke into a big smile. "Never seen the like!" she said proudly. Then she carefully stamped and initialed it back by the stove where we couldn't see.

"Best of luck," said the cook. She handed the mat back facedown. Madame Gulbenkian quickly stuffed it into her purse, got off her stool, shot us a nasty grin, and waddled to her car.

But I'd been too fast for her. Just before the cook slid the place mat across the counter, I had dropped a quarter to the ground and pretended to look for it. Actually, I was really looking up at Madame Gulbenkian's place mat. It went by so fast, I didn't have time to count all the little stamps precisely.

63

But I could tell things didn't look good for us. There was no doubt about it. She was ahead of us by at least twenty meals, and it might've been even more.

"Did you see it?" said Dr. Prechtwinkle, moving over beside me.

I wasn't sure how to break the news. I just nodded.

"How's she doing?" he asked.

"Pretty good."

"But we're still ahead, right?"

"I wouldn't put it just that way."

"How would you put it?"

"We're in trouble," I said. "We're losing!"

I had said the magic word. Dr. Prechtwinkle turned bright red. "Simmer down, simmer down," said the cook. "What you need is a nice soothing bagful of chicken!"

13

I apologized for saying the *L* word. But Dr. Prechtwinkle just sighed. He actually ordered a Roosta-Cola. He looked beaten.

"We are in big trouble," he groaned.

I handed the cook our official place mat. "Very impressive," said she. "Never seen one of these with so many stamps on it."

Dr. Prechtwinkle's face brightened a little.

"Except for that woman's just now," she added.

Dr. Prechtwinkle's gloom came back double.

"Does she have a lot more than we do?" I asked.

"Put it this way: You fellows have a good chance for that second prize."

Dr. Prechtwinkle moaned as though someone had dropped an unabridged dictionary on his left big toe.

"How can she get around the country so fast, anyhow?" I asked.

"Anyone who will break the speed limit will stop at nothing," my cousin said.

"What do we do now?" I asked.

"Keep on! Try harder! We're not licked yet! Maybe she'll get sick. Maybe she'll go to jail for speeding. Maybe she'll lose her appetite. Maybe I'll get the RemDem^{tm} fixed."

"That's an awful lot of maybe's," I said.

Dr. Prechtwinkle didn't reply. He looked awfully thoughtful and awfully sad.

Then someone sat down on the stool beside him and asked the cook, "Do you by any chance have Minnesota pheasant in sauce of Maine lobster?"

There was only one person I knew who sounded like that. "Very funny, kid," the cook replied. "What'll it be?"

"A hot dog, I guess," said my best friend Donald. "Medium rare with just a touch of mustard and a tickle of relish."

"Donald!" I shouted across Dr. Prechtwinkle. "I thought you were running around the world hunting monsters!"

"Oscar! Didn't you get my cards?"

"Just one from Loch Ness."

"Loch Ness! Don't remind me. The first time they

66

tried the submarine, it sank right to the bottom and didn't come up. Lucky for us they were testing it by remote control."

"That wouldn't have been the Prechtwinkle MonsterSub, would it?" my cousin inquired.

I was already sure I knew the answer. "That's the one, all right," Donald said.

"Good thing the warranty expired last April," Dr. Prechtwinkle muttered to himself.

"Anyhow," Donald went on, "all we saw in Transylvania was potatoes and Communists. Dracula's castle was closed. They're remodeling it into a motel or something."

"Pretty disappointing."

"It got worse. The only abominable thing in the Himalayas was the bathroom. By the time we got back to the United States, I'd had it. The closest we came to Bigfoot was a fake cement pawprint. It wasn't a trip, it was a gyp! The only monsters I ever got to see were the toy stuffed ones at the souvenir stands. A week ago, I left a note with the tour leader and phoned my folks to tell them not to worry, and I've been traveling on my own ever since. It's easy if you have money."

"I guess so."

"I'm amazed you didn't get my cards. I must've sent you two dozen. If there was one thing I had plenty of, it was spare time."

"Well, I've been on the road myself," I said.

"What happened to that miserable summer you

were going to have working for that doofus cousin of yours?"

My cousin made a face.

"Donald," I said. "I want you to meet my cousin, Dr. Peter Prechtwinkle."

Donald shook my cousin's hand and said he didn't look like a doofus at all.

14

"Wow!" Donald said, once I'd filled him in about my vacation. "And you were worried about having a rotten summer!"

"Come on!" my cousin shouted from the door of the Picklemobile. "If we don't hit the road, we'll never catch up!"

"Can I come with you?" Donald asked.

Dr. Prechtwinkle gave him a dirty look. "Just what I need. Another mouth to feed."

"Oh, I can pay my own way," said Donald. He took out his wallet. "I've got money and traveler's checks and credit cards and more where that came from. I'm rich."

"You wouldn't happen to have a hundred thousand dollars or so you could spare, would you?"

Donald shook his head. "Not for a while yet. I can't get at my real money until I turn twenty-one."

"What do you think?" Dr. Prechtwinkle asked me.

"I think it'd be neat."

"I might even be able to help you out with this Madame Whatever-Her-Name-Is," Donald said. "I know all about curses and voodoo and stuff like that."

"We're all out of bunks," Dr. Prechtwinkle said. "You'll have to get yourself a sleeping bag."

"I've got one," said Donald. "Mount Everest Custom. Stuffed with yak hair."

"Well, quit yakking and get your stuff up here, then," said my cousin. "And hurry up about it." He helped Donald hoist his gold-mesh duffel bag into the Picklemobile. And we were off!

Donald really liked riding in the Picklemobile. The pickle jokes we'd heard a million times were all new to him. And he kept going "Hey! Hey!" in time with my cousin's polka tape. He hadn't heard it enough yet to be sick of it.

Late that afternoon we arrived at Medical Lake, Washington. The Doctor Chicken Restaurant had a statue of Bagthorpe dressed up like a doctor. The TV antenna was shaped like a stethoscope.

My cousin gave me some money and told us to go in and eat. He stayed outside to work on the Rem-

71

Dem^{tm}. He said if he didn't get it fixed soon, we were sunk.

"What's a RemDem^{tm}?" Donald asked. I explained it to him while we waited for our chicken.

"Going anywhere in the world in a flash sounds like a great idea," he said. "How come he can't get the RemDem^{tm} to work?"

"He can't get anything to work," I said. "His helicopter didn't fly. His Transmo blew up Madame Gulbenkian's house. And you saw what happened to his submarine."

"How about the Picklemobile? That works!"

"Because my cousin didn't invent it. He bought it. Cheap. The one part that doesn't work is the RemDem^{tm}."

"Cluck, cluck! It's in the bag!" said our waitress, who was dressed up in a lab coat and a forehead reflector. It was Donald's first Chicken in the Bag, and he loved it. He couldn't understand why I was just sort of picking at mine.

When we got back to the parking lot, Dr. Prechtwinkle slid out from underneath the Picklemobile. "No luck," he muttered. "No luck at all. I'm going to take a shower. Be ready to leave in a few minutes." He went inside and shut the door.

"Hey, look!" said Donald.

"Look at what?" I asked.

Donald pointed. "That plug and socket on the side of the Picklemobile. He left them apart. Kind of dangling there."

"Typical," I said.

"May as well fix them," Donald suggested.

"I don't know. Maybe he left them that way for a reason."

"Don't be silly," Donald said. He went over and plugged the two parts together. Then he leaned against the Picklemobile. "See?"

The only thing I saw was that the Picklemobile was sort of fading away.

15

In most books, somebody would say "What hap-pened?" But we both knew instantly what had hap-pened.

"It worked!" we shouted at exactly the same time. The loose plug Donald had fixed was the one thing keeping the Picklemobile from turning into the RemDem^{tm}. By now it had disappeared completely.

"Now we have a chance!" I realized. "We'll be able to zip around the country and beat Madame Gulbenkian."

"Not so fast," said Donald. "All we know so far is that the RemDem^{tm} *de*materialized. We have no idea if it *re*materialized."

I suddenly felt glum again. "Yeah. Or where."

"This definitely has to be the weirdest shower your cousin has ever taken. One minute he's soaping up in Medical Lake, Washington. The next he's drying off who knows where. Will he ever be surprised!"

"What do we do now?" I asked.

Donald shrugged. "Beats me."

"I can't believe it'll actually work right," I said. "Maybe he'll rematerialize someplace else and won't be able to get back here at all."

"Well, at least you wouldn't have to eat any more chicken."

All of a sudden I felt a mild bump against my arm. "Look out!" Donald shouted.

I jumped out of the way. The RemDem^{tm} was rematerializing exactly where I was standing.

First it was transparent, so you could see right through it. Then it was kind of shimmery. Then it sort of popped into being its good old warty Picklemobile self again. Dr. Prechtwinkle jumped out and tossed a snowball at us.

"Where'd you get that?" Donald shouted.

"From the top of the Matterhorn in the Swiss Alps!" cried my cousin. "The RemDem^{tm} is working exactly the way it's supposed to! We're going to beat Madame Gulbenkian to that prize after all! Come on! Get in!"

We got in. Dr. Prechtwinkle checked our place mat for a destination clear across the country. He

75

typed it in on the keyboard. The panel on the sun visor flashed **OPA-LOCKA FLORIDA**. Dr. Prechtwinkle pulled the big red lever. Loud rumbling noises came from the back. Curtains slid closed over all the windows. Dr. Prechtwinkle warned us not to look out.

DEMATERIALIZING . . . flashed the panel. Then **REMATERIALIZING** . . . Then the rumbling quieted down. The panel flashed **YOU'RE THERE!** The curtains slid back. We saw faint palm trees shimmering before our eyes.

"This is the hard part," said Dr. Prechtwinkle as he pushed the lever slowly forward.

"How come?" asked Donald.

"Watch," said my cousin. He slowly eased up on the lever. The palm trees became clearer, almost solid. Then we saw something horrible. We were at the end of an airport runway, and a plane was hurtling straight at us!

Dr. Prechtwinkle pulled the lever hard, and the world disappeared. Then he made a little adjustment on a dial above the keyboard.

"That was a close one," he said.

"I'll say!" Donald agreed.

"With this version, you never know the precise spot where you'll rematerialize. You have to be ready to change your mind in a flash. I'm going to fix that in the next model."

"Good idea," I said.

"You don't want to rematerialize in the middle of a lake, for example, or on top of a tall building, or

even on a downtown street full of cars. And you don't want to attract a lot of attention. You just want a nice peaceful empty place like a deserted parking lot."

He pushed down on the lever again, and the world started coming back into view. "This looks okay," he said. "A big field. Still, you have to be careful."

He checked the mirrors. "Nope," he muttered, and yanked the lever back up again. I could see what he was talking about. We had landed near a sign that said **BUFFALO BERNIE'S BISON BUSINESS**. A stampede was heading our way.

Dr. Prechtwinkle made the tiniest adjustment to

the dial. He gently eased the lever down. When the world came into view again, we were on the safe side of the bison ranch fence. Dr. Prechtwinkle fired up the Picklemobile's normal engine, and we were off to dinner.

"This is fabulous!" Donald said. "We can go anywhere we want. You'll be able to catch up for sure now!"

"Hope you've got a good appetite!" my cousin told me cheerfully. "This may be a seven-Bag day."

I suddenly felt kind of queasy. But Donald insisted there weren't any feathers sprouting from my forehead.

16

Ten Bags was my one-day record. Some days I only had eight or nine, and believe me, that was plenty. Dr. Prechtwinkle wanted me to eat fifteen or twenty. But Donald told him that if he made me eat more than ten a day, he'd have him arrested for cruelty.

Donald told him that because he ate twenty Bags one day himself. He did it just to see if it was possible. It was, but for a couple of days afterward, he just lay around groaning. He didn't eat any more chicken at all after that. He didn't even drink Roosta-Cola.

Still, it was fun having Donald around. He finally

got tired of my cousin's pickle polkas, so he used one of his credit cards to buy a bunch of tapes we liked better. Dr. Prechtwinkle put earplugs in when we played them.

But then I started turning into a chicken again. It was terrible. I had feathers coming out of my forehead and my face and the rest of my body. I couldn't talk. I could only cluck and cackle. I strutted around and pecked for little kernels of dried corn. I knew that soon a farmer would turn up with an axe and start chasing me around the chicken yard. All I could do about it was wake up, since it was only a dream—but it was the scariest dream I'd ever had. And I kept having it over and over again.

Turning into a chicken every night in my dreams wasn't the only new thing I had to worry about, either. Our latest problem started at the Chic'n Boat restaurant in Steamboat Springs, Colorado. The manager was wearing a sailor hat with Bagthorpe on it in gold braid. When I handed him my place mat, he couldn't believe his eyes.

"Lookee, lookee!" he shouted to the people at the counter. "This little fella has done some heavy-duty chicken-chomping!" He waved the place mat in the air.

Almost everybody at the counter came over for a closer look. There were a lot of oohs and aahs. People asked a lot of dumb questions. One of the women told us to stick around. She said she was a TV reporter, and she would put us on the late news.

I thought it would be fun to go on TV. But Dr. Prechtwinkle rushed me out of the place. "The last thing we want is publicity," he said.

"Why?" I asked.

"Because we don't want Madame Gulbenkian to find out where we are and try to turn you into a chicken again. Or worse."

"How can she follow us?" Donald asked. "We can always dematerialize in the RemDem^{tm}."

"You've never met her, lucky for you," said my cousin. "She might use her supernatural powers."

"I told you, I know all about that stuff," Donald bragged. "You're not going to get pains in your toes anymore."

"Maybe not," I said, "but my cousin's right. Madame Gulbenkian can give us a lot bigger pain than that."

That afternoon we walked into the giant egg at Irv's Chick-O-Rama in Thermopolis, Wyoming. Irv welcomed us in as though he'd almost expected us. Somehow he knew I wanted Chicken in the Bag before I even ordered it.

When I was almost done eating, a couple of people came in with a microphone and a TV camera. Then I noticed Irv nod in my direction. "Uh-oh," I said.

"Uh-oh what?" said my cousin.

I pointed. The woman with the camera and the man with the microphone were heading straight for our table.

"Wait a minute! No interviews!" Dr. Prechtwinkle shouted. But the next thing I knew, the camera and microphone were right in my face.

Dr. Prechtwinkle protested, hollered, and complained, but Irv refused to stamp our mat until we cooperated. So I had to play along. I had to stick an extra chicken leg in my mouth just for the camera. I had to hold up my place mat and point to the stamps. I had to smile at Irv while he made a big deal out of stamping and initialing the mat.

We saw the report that night over our late snack at The Chicken Windmill in Dutch John, Utah. Irv said that I was the most important person who ever came into his restaurant, and that if I won the contest, he would frame my autograph and the Polaroid picture he took of me.

"I'm glad that's over," I said. But it wasn't. The owner of The Chicken Windmill was already on the phone to his local TV station. He refused to stamp our place mat until we posed with him out front beneath the giant chicken feathers turning in the wind.

Word got around fast. All the Chicken in the Bag places were on alert for us. It got so bad that most of the time the TV crews would show up before my order did.

Dr. Prechtwinkle thought we might sneak through by using disguises. He bought me a false moustache and a green alpine hat with a feather. He wore a toupee and a putty nose. He made Donald wear a fake beard and phony ears.

The first time we tried it, my moustache kept slipping, and I nearly swallowed it. Donald's beard landed in his soup. My cousin's nose fell off and clattered to the floor. And when we handed over my place mat to be stamped, the owner recognized it and kept us waiting till the TV people got there.

That was the end of the disguises. We just hoped Madame Gulbenkian wouldn't see one of the news reports. We asked about her everywhere we went. Nobody seemed to remember her. We figured she must have covered this part of the country before her place mat had enough stamps to attract attention.

After my ninth Bag of August 16, there was still no sign of her. Better yet, we were down to just eleven missing Bagthorpe stamps. Just eleven more bags of chicken, and the prize would be ours.

"Wow! I can't believe we're that close already," said Donald as we dematerialized near Happy Union, Texas.

"That's because you haven't been eating the chicken," I said.

"Let me see the place mat," he said.

I handed it over. Donald looked at it carefully. "Wait a second. I count *twelve* Chicken in the Bags without stamps," said Donald.

"The one in Squantz, Connecticut, doesn't count," Dr. Prechtwinkle explained. "It had its franchise taken away." And we told Donald all about the two Als.

Donald counted the missing stamps one last time just to make sure. "Eleven it is," he said as we rematerialized next to a grain silo. "One more tonight. Ten tomorrow."

There was a TV above the counter in the next place. As I was finishing my chicken, I heard a familiar voice screech, "I am going to be winner, you bet!"

Dr. Prechtwinkle shuddered and turned toward the screen. There was Madame Gulbenkian. She swallowed a whole chicken leg in one gulp.

"Is that . . . ?" Donald asked.

"Shhh!" Dr. Prechtwinkle interrupted.

"Just five more Bags, and I win, you bet," said
Madame Gulbenkian with a big smile.

It took us ten minutes to revive Dr. Prechtwinkle
after he fainted.

17

"We can still win," Donald said next morning. "The TV said she was somewhere in the South, and she still had a couple of places to get to in New England. And then she has to get back to Texas to claim the prize. Even if she uses airplanes to get around, she can't do all that in one day."

But we had ten Bags to go in ten different states. And of course, that's when the RemDem^{tm} decided to act up. Every time we dematerialized, it took longer and longer to rematerialize again. The third time we rematerialized, it was like waiting for the sun to come up.

"It's the big distances," Dr. Prechtwinkle said. "They're putting a strain on the RemDem^{tm}."

I suddenly had a scary thought. "What happens if there's something wrong and we can't rematerialize?"

"Highly unlikely," said Dr. Prechtwinkle. "Almost impossible."

A cornfield slowly faded into view.

"But what if?" Donald asked.

"We'd be stuck," said Dr. Prechtwinkle.

"Where?" Donald inquired. "In the middle of nowhere?"

Dr. Prechtwinkle nodded. "Neither here nor there."

"And then what?" I asked.

"We could get out and push," Donald said.

"Very funny," said Dr. Prechtwinkle, easing the lever down as the cornfield outside finally began to look solid. "But it can't happen. No chance. I built in a special system for just such emergencies."

But Donald and I knew all about my cousin's inventions. We breathed a sigh of relief as the indicator on the visor changed from **REMATERIALIZING** . . . to **YOU'RE THERE!**

The tenth time we dematerialized that day, it took us nearly half an hour to rematerialize. By the time the **YOU'RE THERE!** sign finally flashed at us, we were half convinced we must be in the middle of nowhere.

But we weren't. We were in Cadillac, Michigan, right where we were supposed to be. And that's where I ate my 210th bag of chicken.

It was all over. I was through with chicken for

good. When the TV reporters left, Donald and Dr. Prechtwinkle shook my hand and slapped me on the back. You can't believe how great I felt.

"I'll never eat chicken again as long as I live," I said.

"Never?" Donald asked.

"Never."

"Not even if you were marooned on a desert island with a bunch of chickens?"

"I'd eat the bark off trees. I'd eat beetles. I'd eat worms. The chickens would be safe."

All we had to do now was go to Chicken in the Bag International Headquarters to collect the prize. But the office wouldn't be open till morning. So Dr. Prechtwinkle decided to let the RemDem^{tm} and everybody else have a good night's rest before we traveled to Henrietta, Texas.

I dreamed a lot that night. First I dreamed I was a human being in a chicken suit. As far as I was concerned, that was a real improvement over my usual dreams.

Then I dreamed of breakfast, a normal breakfast on a normal china plate. No more bags and no more chicken for me! I had pancakes and waffles and bacon and home-fried potatoes. But when the waitress brought me some eggs, I sent them back. They were a little too close to chicken for comfort.

18

Dr. Prechtwinkle was underneath the Picklemobile at the crack of dawn. He was tinkering with the RemDem™ again.

"I just hope he knows what he's doing," I said.

"He did invent this, after all," said Donald.

"I know," I said. "That's what scares me."

But my cousin insisted everything was fine. We were planning to travel to Henrietta, Texas, and have a great breakfast. Then we would go off to claim our prize.

"And won't Madame You-Know-Who be mad!" said Donald.

Then my cousin started up the RemDem™. It didn't rumble at all. It just kind of creaked. The scenery outside took forever to fade away, and the curtains just kind of crawled shut. The **DEMATERI-ALIZING** . . . message on the little screen on the sun visor blinked very slowly, too. And instead of changing to **REMATERIALIZING** . . . the screen just went blank.

"We're not going to get stuck in the middle of nowhere, are we?" I asked.

Dr. Prechtwinkle didn't say a word. He looked at his watch. He tapped his fingers on the dashboard. He jiggled the lever. He jostled the sun visor. Nothing happened.

Donald and I looked at each other. We both expected the worst. When an hour and fifteen minutes had gone by, Donald whispered to me, "We're stuck!"

My cousin just stood there and shook his head. Finally he had had enough. "Come on, you stupid machine! Work!" he hollered.

Letter by letter, **REMATERIALIZING** . . . appeared on the screen. At least we were getting somewhere. But it still took another awful hour until the letters changed to **YOU'RE THERE!**

And when the curtains crawled open, the world outside was still almost transparent. As it began to solidify, I looked at my watch. Usually the whole thing took about two minutes. This time we had been gone for nearly two hours.

Dr. Prechtwinkle mopped his head with a rag. "I'm definitely going to have to do something to fix this thing."

"What about breakfast?" I asked.

"It's already lunchtime," said my cousin. "The office must be open already. There'll be time enough to eat once we've collected the prize."

As we drove to the address on the place mat, we expected to see a big chicken statue up ahead, the Bagthorpe to end all Bagthorpes. But all we could see was a bunch of ramshackle warehouses and factories. 12 Pinfeather Lane, the address we were looking for, was a shabby old building coated with flaking yellow paint.

The directory in the lobby listed a whole range of fine companies:

1   **CLUCKY CHICKEN FEED, LTD.**
2   **FEATHER YOUR NECK PILLOWS AND SON**
3   **GRUB WORLD**
4   **ROOSTER COMBS, INC.**

And, finally, what we were looking for:

5   **INTERNATIONAL CHICKEN IN THE BAG, INC.**
     —WORLD HEADQUARTERS

The elevator had an **OUT OF ORDER** sign on it, so we had to walk up all five flights. Once we made it to the top, the rest was easy. A faded portrait of Bagthorpe pointed in the right direction. A sign on the door said **CACKLE TWICE AND SCRATCH ON IN!**

Donald did the cackling. My cousin opened the door to a little reception area.

"One moment, please," said a scrawny woman at the front desk. She was talking on the phone. "Yes, sir, Captain. It is a wonderful day in the history of Chicken in the Bag. We're all celebrating wildly here. I can take the day off? Thank you, Captain, sir!"

She hung up the phone and got up from her chair. "It's a red-letter day for us," she said. "A woman in Connecticut is about to win our Chicken in the Bag Bagful o' Cash."

"That can't be!" said Dr. Prechtwinkle. "We've already won!"

The woman looked baffled. "Impossible!" said she. "We're about to award the prize. Just as soon as she eats her 211th bag of chicken."

"But we've already won," said Dr. Prechtwinkle. "Oscar here has eaten at every Chicken in the Bag establishment in the entire United States. We've got the place mat to prove it."

"Not possible. Besides, we're closed. The boss just gave me the rest of the day off."

"We have come to claim our prize," said Dr. Prechtwinkle, "and we won't wait another minute."

He pulled the place mat out of its case and handed it to the woman. She looked amazed. "Oh, my," she said. "You really have gotten around, haven't you?"

"We sure have," I said.

"I think I'd better make a phone call," she said. She went back to her desk and punched a long string of numbers into the phone.

"It won't be long now," Dr. Prechtwinkle told me with a smile. "I'm sure it'll all be straightened out in a jiffy."

"Is Captain Capon still there?" the woman said into the phone. "Put him on the line, please. We have a slight problem."

Donald and I looked at the pictures on the walls. One showed a man in a pirate hat and eye patch standing in front of a giant Bagthorpe that didn't look quite right somehow. At the bottom it said **Captain Capon and Old Number 1**.

"We have a problem, sir," said the woman. "A young fellow just came in here with a full place mat. It certainly looks genuine."

She waited a second. "Yes, every one."

She looked at the place mat. "Where? Oh, *there*. Let me see." She pressed her nose against a spot near the east coast. "You're absolutely correct, sir." She smiled. "I'll tell them. Good-bye, sir."

She put the phone back on the hook. Then she handed the place mat back to us. "That was Captain Capon, our president, chairman, and chief executive officer. He congratulates you for your efforts, and believes you may well be in line for second prize."

"*Second* prize? What?" demanded Dr. Prechtwinkle.

"If you examine the place mat closely, you'll discover that you're missing one stamp."

"Of course," said Dr. Prechtwinkle. "Squantz, Connecticut. You took the franchise away from an outfit called Als. They don't even have the stamps anymore."

"That is quite correct," said the woman. "Als Restaurant has not had the right to serve Chicken in the Bag since January 1 of this year. They refused to maintain our strict quality standards and unusual atmosphere."

"Right," said Dr. Prechtwinkle. "You can't expect

us to get a stamp from a franchise that doesn't exist."

"Of course not. But we do expect you to have the stamp from our new official franchise holder in the Squantz area."

"Uh-oh," said Donald.

"You mean someone else has the franchise?" I asked.

The woman nodded. "A restaurant called Bigfoot."

Dr. Prechtwinkle yanked me by the arm. "Come on! One more meal!"

"Oh, no!" I moaned.

"You're too close to quit now!" Donald said.

"You can't possibly win," said the woman. "Your competition is already on the way to that restaurant. She'll be there in less than half an hour."

"So will we!" Dr. Prechtwinkle declared. "Come on!" And we half ran, half jumped, and I know this makes three halves, but we actually rolled down the stairs partway when Dr. Prechtwinkle tripped and fell and we did, too.

"Get in!" my cousin cried, shoving us into the Picklemobile. He got underneath and banged around for a minute or two. Then he came inside.

"Stand by!" he shouted. We did.

Dr. Prechtwinkle pushed the lever down. Absolutely nothing happened.

Donald looked at me. I looked at Donald. We were both absolutely positive that the RemDem™ had picked this very moment to die.

19

The RemDem™ hadn't died. But it wasn't working exactly right, either.

Dr. Prechtwinkle's banging had gotten it working again. But somehow he'd added a little too much power.

The first time we rematerialized, we were right in the middle of the Atlantic Ocean. My cousin fiddled with the dials a little. Soon we were in Siberia, teetering on the edge of a steep cliff. Then we nearly landed in Chile, Bora Bora, the Aleutian Islands, and New Zealand. But finally Dr. Prechtwinkle cried "Aha!" He fiddled with the dials again.

Thirty seconds later we rematerialized at one end of a field where some kids were playing baseball. A home run just missed our windshield. But the kids told us we were in Squantz, Connecticut.

They also told us the Bigfoot restaurant was clear across town. But the way things were going, even Dr. Prechtwinkle knew better than to try dematerializing again.

So we drove the Picklemobile onto the expressway. That's when we saw Madame Gulbenkian in the distance behind us.

And believe me, she saw us. In the rearview mirrors we could see her waggle her fingers toward us.

"Quick, Donald!" I said.

He leaned out the window and pointed his fingers in her direction. "Bluggle ruggle tuggle!" he shouted.

Madame Gulbenkian drew her hand back as if it had been stung.

"Nice work!" said Dr. Prechtwinkle. "My foot doesn't hurt a bit."

"Mine, neither," I said.

Madame Gulbenkian pointed her other hand at us. "Borgle morgle rorgle!" Donald shouted at her.

Madame Gulbenkian shook her hand as though a mosquito had bitten it.

"Good going!" Dr. Prechtwinkle cried.

We could see the Bigfoot restaurant up ahead. It was shaped like a big chicken foot. And it was decorated for a celebration. A small crowd had gathered outside. Pennants fluttered over the parking lot. A human being dressed up in a Bagthorpe suit jumped up and down to attract attention. And six armed guards stood around looking mean in front of a giant Bagful o' Cash.

Donald and I jumped out of the Picklemobile and ran into the Bigfoot's giant middle toe. "One Chicken in the Bag, please!" I shouted. "And hurry!"

A man in an eyepatch and a pirate hat rushed in right behind us. "Not so fast, you clucks! I'm Captain Capon, and I've got an important event scheduled here."

"You certainly do," said Donald. "He's going to win the Bagful o' Cash!" He waved the place mat under the Captain's nose.

"He is not, you bet!" shouted Madame Gulbenkian, barging through the door. "I am! One Chicken in the Bag!"

"We were here first!" Donald shouted.

Captain Capon suddenly got a gleam in the one eye you could see. "We'll have an eat-off!" he cried. "You'll both get your chicken at exactly the same time. May the best chicken-eater win!"

"It's all over now," I muttered to Donald.

Captain Capon sat me down at one side of a table and put a Bagthorpe bib around my neck. Then he sat Madame Gulbenkian directly across from me and fastened her bib.

She waggled her fingers at me. I expected my toe to throb, but before it did, Donald waggled right back and shouted "Blaggle raggle mctaggle!"

Madame Gulbenkian grabbed her left elbow as though it had been hit by a bolt of lightning. "Where did you learn that?" she screeched.

"Never you mind!" said Donald. "That'll teach you to pick on my friend's toes."

"You'd better not try that again, sonny!" she shouted.

"Yeah, cool it," I told Donald. "There's no telling what she might try if she got really angry."

"I'll handle her," Donald told me. "You just concentrate on winning."

"That's easy for you to say," I said. "You've never seen her eat."

The air was filled with the smell of Chicken in the Bag as Dr. Prechtwinkle came through the door. "Don't turn chicken now!" he shouted at me. All I could think of was that Donald's powers had better keep on working, or Madame Gulbenkian might make my forehead sprout feathers again.

"Two Bags, coming right up!" Captain Capon declared. Two waitresses set them on the tables at exactly the same time. We were off and eating!

"Come on!" Dr. Prechtwinkle hollered. "Wolf that chicken!"

I tried. I really did. But before I even finished my wing, Madame Gulbenkian was done with her breast and halfway through her leg. Dr. Prechtwinkle urged me on, but his voice was getting fainter.

I chewed less and swallowed more. But I was just starting on my leg. Madame Gulbenkian had already munched her way through her thigh. I could see Dr. Prechtwinkle's eyes begin to fill with tears.

Suddenly someone burst through the door and shouted, "Now, sister, I will have my revenge!"

I looked up. It was Juanita Frye. Madame Gulbenkian made an ugly face at her.

"Don't worry about them!" Donald told me. "Just keep eating!"

I tried, but I knew I was licked. All Madame Gulbenkian had left was the tiny wing. The only way I could win would be to swallow the rest of my chicken whole, bones and all.

"I saw your evil face on TV!" Juanita Frye shouted at her twin. "But your dastardly plans won't succeed this time!" She waggled her fingers at her sister and shouted a few strange words.

Madame Gulbenkian began hiccuping so wildly she dropped her chicken wing in her lap.

"Now, come on, kid!" Ms. Frye shouted at me. "You can do it!"

"Sure you can!" Donald cried.

The hiccups were definitely slowing Madame Gulbenkian down. I tore into my chicken breast as fast as I could.

Madame Gulbenkian drank some water to try to stop her hiccups. It didn't help. But hiccups or no hiccups, she was determined to finish that chicken wing. She took a deep breath and swallowed hard.

I was catching up, but Madame Gulbenkian was down to her last nibble. She stopped just to give me a look of triumph. "Too—hic—bad, sonny!" she crowed. But just as she was about to put the wing into her mouth again, someone came through the door and hollered "Stop!"

Madame Gulbenkian turned to look.

"Whatever you do, keep eating!" Donald whispered to me.

"I have eaten everywhere!" said the person at the door. It was Al the First. "I win!"

"Hic—what?" cried Madame Gulbenkian.

"We have not been affiliated with Chicken in the Bag since January 1, and Al here just won the contest over in Old Haven," said Al the Second. "We've got the place mat to prove it."

"Let me see that," said Captain Capon. He grabbed the place mat from Al the Second's hand.

I just kept eating. I didn't know if my stomach could handle it, but I was wolfing down food faster than any wolf that ever lived.

"This seems to be in order," said Captain Capon.

"It can't—hic—be!" cried Madame Gulbenkian, and got up to see for herself. Then she remembered to finish the last bite of her chicken. Either way, I had lost.

"Stamp my—hic—mat!" cried Madame Gulbenkian.

"Congratulations. You'll win second prize," said Al the First.

"Keep on eating," Donald whispered to me.

"Impostors!" cried Madame Gulbenkian. She gave the Als an evil stare.

"Ow!" they shouted, grabbing their feet.

I polished off the breast, then made short work of the wing. I was done. But I hadn't even won second prize. Dr. Prechtwinkle would have to hand over his mansion and all his inventions.

Worse, Madame Gulbenkian had come in second. She wouldn't win anything but a year's supply of Chicken in the Bag. There was no doubt she'd try to turn my cousin into a microwave oven. I felt like throwing up.

Dr. Prechtwinkle was sitting with his head in his hands and sobbing. Once in a while he looked up at Madame Gulbenkian and sobbed louder.

"Stamp Oscar's place mat!" Donald said.

Captain Capon finished stamping Madame Gulbenkian's mat. Then he stamped mine. "Looks like you're in third place, laddie," said he. "Better luck next time."

"Not so fast!" Donald said.

"Huh?" replied everybody else except Dr. Prechtwinkle, who was still crying his eyes out.

Donald pointed to the place mat. "The official rules say you have to bring the winning place mat with all necessary certifications to International Chicken in the Bag World Headquarters in Henrietta, Texas."

"But I'm the president of Chicken in the Bag International, and I'm here right now," said Captain Capon.

"That doesn't make any difference," Donald said. "Rules are rules."

"Let me see that," said Captain Capon irritably. He grabbed my place mat from my hands and stared at it. Out of the corner of my eye, I noticed Madame Gulbenkian sneaking out the door.

"It really does say that, I'm afraid," said Captain Capon.

At the exact same instant, Donald yelled, "Stop her!"

But we were too late. Madame Gulbenkian waddled outside in the fastest hurry of her life. Then she climbed aboard the Picklemobile, hiccuped, and slammed the door.

20

We all ran toward the Picklemobile in a human wave—Donald, Dr. Prechtwinkle, Captain Capon, both Als, Juanita Frye, people from the TV stations, and everybody else hanging around. But we were too late. Through the windshield we could see Madame Gulbenkian pull the lever back. An instant later, the Picklemobile began to fade away.

"Stand back!" Dr. Prechtwinkle shouted, and the human wave stopped in its tracks. But Donald kept running.

Dr. Prechtwinkle hid his head in his hands. The Picklemobile was fading fast. It was almost invisible.

But Donald ran right up to it. He grabbed the wire

he had fixed days ago. He gave it a hard yank. The little plug came out of the little socket. The engines stopped roaring.

The Picklemobile became totally invisible anyway.

Donald said a couple of words my parents wouldn't want anybody to know I knew. I said them, too. The Als and Ms. Frye just stood there gaping. And Captain Capon asked if anybody could tell him what was going on.

I had no idea. But there was this strange shimmering in the space where the Picklemobile used to be. You could see right through it, but it was sort of wavy, like the hot air above a candle.

"Can anybody tell me what is going on around here?" Captain Capon repeated.

Dr. Prechtwinkle took his head out of his hands and looked up. "How long has it been shimmering like that?"

"About a minute or so," said Donald.

"What happened?"

"I pulled the plug just before it faded away."

"Amazing!" Dr. Prechtwinkle laughed wildly. "Fantastic!" He shook Donald's hand again and again. "The RemDem^{tm} is suspended in time and space. And so is Madame Gulbenkian. Serves her right!"

"Huh?" everybody but Donald and me said all at once.

"It's extremely complicated," said my cousin.

And he explained all about how he had invented the RemDem^{tm} and how it could dematerialize in one place and rematerialize somewhere else.

"Would you get to the point?" Captain Capon demanded.

"Once the RemDem^{tm} begins dematerializing," said Dr. Prechtwinkle, "it needs a steady supply of power to be able to rematerialize again."

"I get it," said Donald. "And when I pulled the plug, that cut the power."

"Right. Of course, it must have coasted a bit while it was powering down. Otherwise it wouldn't have turned invisible."

"Does that mean Madame Gulbenkian will be stuck in the middle of nowhere forever?" I asked.

"Neither here nor there?" Donald added.

"That sounds pretty awful," said Juanita Frye. "Even for my twin sister, even if she did try to steal your pickle thing."

"No need to worry," said Dr. Prechtwinkle. "When I invented the RemDem^{tm}, I thought of every possibility. Pretty soon now, the machine will switch to auxiliary power and rematerialize automatically right here."

"When she does, we'll arrest her on charges of attempting to steal a vehicle," said one of the policemen. "That is a vehicle, isn't it?"

"It's a terrific vehicle," I said proudly.

"Two vehicles in one," Dr. Prechtwinkle pointed out.

"Just make sure everybody stands back, so nobody ends up getting squashed when it rematerializes," Donald said.

"Well, I guess there's nothing to do now but wait around," said Captain Capon.

"We're not waiting for anybody," said Al the Second. "We're heading for Henrietta, Texas, to claim that prize."

"Second prize, I'm afraid," said Dr. Prechtwinkle cheerfully. "There's no way you'll beat the Rem-Dem^{tm}. We'll be there in five minutes."

"Impossible," said Al the First.

"Can't be," said Al the Second.

"Captain, if you'd like to save yourself a long trip, you're welcome to join us," said my cousin.

"I don't know if I believe what you're saying about that contraption, either," said Captain Capon suspiciously. He lifted his eye patch to stare at the shimmering spot with both eyes. "Where is it, anyway?"

Dr. Prechtwinkle looked at his watch. "I'd say it should be fading back in about one minute." But as he finished his sentence, the Picklemobile began to turn solid again. "It's an experimental model," said my cousin. "We still have a few minor adjustments to make."

"Arrest that woman!" shouted one of the policemen as Madame Gulbenkian stepped out of the Picklemobile. She hiccuped and waggled her fingers in all directions.

"Ow! My toe!" cried half a dozen people in the

108

crowd, including the policeman closest to her. But that didn't stop him from putting the handcuffs around her wrists.

"Where did you learn that hiccup curse?" Donald asked Ms. Frye.

"It's the one thing my uncle taught me," she said.

"We can do that just with our cooking," remarked Al the Second.

My cousin opened the door to the RemDem™. "Would you care to join us, Captain?"

"This thing really works?" Captain Capon said.

"It sure does," said Donald.

"We'll see you in a few days, I guess, Captain," said Al the Second glumly.

"Oh, look at it this way," said Al the First. "At least with that second prize, we won't have to eat our own cooking for a year."

You probably read the rest in the papers. We landed in Henrietta, Texas, about five minutes later, and I claimed the prize. I had to give most of it to Dr. Prechtwinkle. He had to give most of that to Madame Gulbenkian. She'll be able to rebuild her house in a couple of months when she gets out of jail for stealing the Picklemobile and RemDem™.

Chicken in the Bag got a lot of publicity. You can find it almost everywhere now. Donald says it doesn't taste as good as it used to ever since Captain Capon sold out to some big company that's famous for its detergent, toothpaste, and toilet bowl cleaner.

But now you can buy Bagthorpe dolls, Bagthorpe stickers, Bagthorpe frying pans, and even Bagthorpe microwave ovens. Captain Capon has been on all the major talk shows and the cover of *People* magazine. It recently reported that he and Madame Gulbenkian's twin sister are planning to get married.

Donald got his parents to invest in my cousin's latest invention, monster repellent. The idea is that if you wear it while you sleep, no monster will come near you. Dr. Prechtwinkle has already tested it on hundreds of people. Not one has been attacked by a monster, if you don't count big mosquitoes and killer bees.

It's too bad about the RemDem^{tm}, though. Dr. Prechtwinkle forgot to set the parking brake one evening. The next morning, the Picklemobile was at the bottom of the swamp. When they dredged it out, the RemDem^{tm} was ruined for good.

As for me, I put my winnings into my bank account. The giant paper sack is in my bedroom. I sit inside it when I don't want anybody to bother me.

You can look in any record book for this year and find my name listed as the World Champion Chicken-Eater. But you'll have to look fast. Next year, Chicken in the Bag is planning an even bigger and better contest. I am not planning to enter.

ABOUT THE AUTHOR

STEPHEN MANES is an author, journalist, and screenwriter. He has published more than twenty-five books, including *The Boy Who Turned Into a TV Set*, the *Hooples* series, and the first two books in the Oscar Noodleman series —*That Game From Outer Space* and *The Oscar J. Noodleman Television Network*. His *The Obnoxious Jerks* is available in a Bantam Starfire hardcover edition; *It's New! It's Improved! It's Terrible!* and the award-winning *Be a Perfect Person in Just Three Days!* are available in Bantam Skylark editions.

Mr. Manes is a contributing editor and regular columnist for *PC Magazine*. He codeveloped Bantam's *StarFixer* software and wrote *The Complete MCI Mail Handbook*. With *Chicken Trek*'s illustrator Ron Barrett he created *Encyclopedia Placematica*, the world's first book of place mats. He and his books have been the subject of several television programs.

ABOUT THE ILLUSTRATOR

RON BARRETT says that he researched the pictures for *Chicken Trek* by looking at pictures of cooked chicken. He has illustrated many books, including *Cloudy With A Chance Of Meatballs* by Judi Barrett. He lives and works in New York City.

Wild and crazy adventures from
<u>Stephen Manes!</u>

☐ **BE A PERFECT PERSON IN
JUST THREE DAYS!** 15580-6 $2.95

Milo Crinkley tries to follow the loony instructions on being perfect, found in a library book. But who ever heard of wearing a stalk of broccoli around your neck for twenty-four hours? And that's only the first day...

☐ **IT'S NEW! IT'S IMPROVED!
IT'S TERRIBLE!**   15682-9 $2.75

The TV commercials say the shoes that basketball star Ralph "Helicopter" Jones wears are "New! IMPROVED! Amazing! NEAT!" Arnold Schlemp just has to have them. At least until the commercial steps out of his TV set and into his life!

☐ **CHICKEN TREK**   15716-7 $2.75

Oscar Noodleman spends his summer vacation entering the "Chicken in the Bag" contest and eating 211 chicken meals at restaurants across America! But Oscar's not the only one after the $99,999.99 prize. Join the Chicken Trek!

Buy them at your local bookstore or use this page to order:

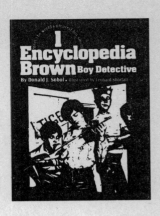

SKYLARK BOOKS
can be *your* special friends

☐ 15615 **THE WHITE STALLION** by Elizabeth Shub. $2.75 ($3.25 in Canada) Long ago, a proud white stallion roamed the plains of Texas. Cowboys said he was the greatest horse that ever lived. Gretchen discovers, in a scary, exciting adventure, that they were right.

☐ 15777 **JACK GALAXY, SPACE COP** by Robert Kraus. $2.75 ($3.25 in Canada) Jack zooms through the universe fighting space crime with his best friend Sally and Jojo the space dog. Giant hamburgers are taking over the world and only Jack & his friends can save the day!

☐ 15711 **BUMPS IN THE NIGHT** by Harry Allard. $2.50 ($2.95 in Canada) Dudley the Stork finds out his new house is haunted and is determined to find out just who the ghost is.

Buy them wherever paperback books are sold—or order below.

CHOOSE YOUR OWN ADVENTURE®

SKYLARK EDITIONS

☐ 15744	**Circus #1**	$2.50
☐ 15679	**Haunted House #2**	$2.50
☐ 15680	**Green Slime #6**	$2.50
☐ 15562	**Summer Camp #18**	$2.50
☐ 15732	**Haunted Harbor #33**	$2.50
☐ 15453	**Haunted Halloween Party #37**	$2.50
☐ 15492	**The Great Easter Adventure #40**	$2.50
☐ 15742	**The Movie Mystery #41**	$2.50
☐ 15709	**Home in Time for Christmas #43**	$2.50
☐ 15612	**Day With Dinosaurs #46**	$2.50
☐ 15672	**Spooky Thanksgiving #47**	$2.50
☐ 15685	**You Are Invisible #48**	$2.50
☐ 15696	**Race of the Year #49**	$2.75
☐ 15762	**Stranded! #50**	$2.75
☐ 15776	**You Can Make a Difference: The Story of Martin Luther King, Jr.**	$2.50